N.E. Colby is a wife and stay at home mom who home-schools her two children, using mixed media to enhance their lessons. She has always loved animals, and through documentaries and excursions to the zoo, has instilled a love of animals in her children. It is that love that inspired her to create stories about animals for children to read and enjoy!

i

Zoo Vet
AND
THE OTTER

by

N.E. Colby

AUSTIN MACAULEY PUBLISHERS™
LONDON * CAMBRIDGE * NEW YORK * SHARJAH

Copyright © N.E. Colby (2018)

Ordering Information:
Quantity sales: special discounts are available on quantity purchases by corporations, associations, and others. For details, contact the publisher at the address below.

Colby, N.E.
Zoo Vet and the Otter

ISBN 9781641827553 (Paperback)
ISBN 9781641827560 (Hardback)
ISBN 9781641827577 (E-Book)

The main category of the book — Family & relationships

www.austinmacauley.com/us

First Published (2018)
Austin Macauley Publishers LLC
40 Wall Street, 28th Floor
New York, NY 10005
USA

mail-usa@austinmacauley.com
+1 (646) 5125767

My children, who are my whole world. Thank you for making me a better person.
I love you so much!

To my husband and sister; thank you both for your unwavering support and encouragement.
I love you both!

As kids enter the zoo to see all the fantastic animals, the **zoo's** veterinarian visits the playful Tamarins. **Dr. Logan** loves watching them eat their vegetables and bugs.

"Look," A girl says.

"How silly are those otters." She says with a smile. **Dr. Logan** asks the kids, "Did you know there are thirteen species of otters and the largest species is the Giant Otter who can grow over five feet?"

Logan waves to the otters. One of them isn't waving back.
Hm, **Dr. Logan** thinks, *that one's holding his paw.*
I wonder if he's hurt.

Behind the enclosure, he sees the **Zoo** Keeper.

"Hi, **Scarlett**."

"**Dr. Logan!**" Scarlett says. "I'm glad you're here. **Leonard** slipped off the rock and hurt his paw. Can you help him?"

"I sure can." **Dr. Logan** leads **Leonard** into a carrier.

"To the clinic for a checkup, we go!"

Dr. Logan checks **Leonard's** eyes, inside his ears, and his heart, *thump, thump*. Everything there is okay.

Next, **Dr. Logan** carefully checks **Leonard's** front paw.

"**Zoo** Keeper **Scarlett** said you slipped off a big rock and it looks like you sprained your paw pretty bad, **Leonard**. Don't worry. I'll wrap it in a bandage and soon it'll be good as new."

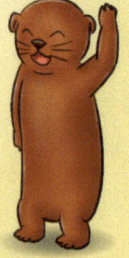

A few days later, **Scarlett** goes to the Vet's office.

"How's your patient, **Dr. Logan**?"

"**Leonard**," **Logan** says, "Say hello to **Zoo** Keeper **Scarlett**."

Leonard waves hello to **Scarlett**.

"Wow!" **Scarlett** Says. "He looks all fixed up. Great job."

Logan smiles. "He's feeling much better."

"Could this happen to the other otters?" **Scarlett** asks.

"It's possible." **Logan** says. "Maybe we should take the rocks out of their habitat."

"We can't do that." **Scarlett** states. "Rocks are an important part of their natural environment."

"Hm," **Logan** thinks. "We can't take away the rocks.
And the ones we have are too big. Sounds like we need…"
"Smaller rocks!"

Back at the otter **habitat**, Logan and Scarlett wave goodbye to Leonard.

"Want to know a fun fact, sis?" Logan asks.

"What?"

"I love our zoo."

"Me too."

The end